THE TEENY, TINY WITCHES

Weekly Reader Children's Book Club presents

THE TEENY, TINY WITCHES

by Jan Wahl
illustrated by Margot Tomes

G. P. Putnam's Sons / New York

Copyright © 1979 by Jan Wahl
Illustrations Copyright © 1979 by Margot Tomes
All rights reserved. Published simultaneously in
Canada by Longman Canada Limited, Toronto.
PRINTED IN THE UNITED STATES OF AMERICA.

Library of Congress Cataloging in Publication Data
Wahl, Jan.
The teeny, tiny witches
SUMMARY: Relates the adventures of a family of
teeny tiny witches as they search for a home.
[Witches—Fiction] I. Tomes, Margot. II. Title.
PZ7.W1226Te   [E]   78-15657
ISBN 0-399-61170-3

For Sara, the good white witch

There are all kinds of witches.

Mean witches. Kind witches. Fat witches.

Skinny witches. Cross witches.

And happy witches.

But there was only one family

of teeny tiny witches.

Ma Witch and Pa Witch

and their small son Sam Witch.

They had just moved into a pumpkin,
lying orange and green in a field.
Pa Witch cut little windows and a door.
Ma Witch helped scoop out
the slippery insides.
And Sam Witch played nearby
with an acorn.

At night the pumpkin was lit
with a cheery glow.
Pa Witch smoked his pipe.
Pa was happy
with their new little home.

But one cold morning
a shrew family pushed its way in,
pushing out Ma, Pa, small Sam,
and all their furniture.
"If only we could make magic
like other witches. We would
show those shrews a thing or two,"
said Pa.
But they were too tiny.
"Now we must start all over again."

Pa groaned. "Where can we fit in?"
"We might fit in there," said Ma Witch.
She pointed to a hole in a hickory tree.
They fixed it into a comfortable,
cozy house. It was a lot of work,
but it was worth it.

When the wind blew,
and the giant owl hooted on a limb,
they were safe and snug.
Ma Witch stitched a picture
in needlepoint.
It said HOME SWEET HOME.

Leaves turned brown and brittle.
One brisk fall morning
two squirrels dumped a load of walnuts
and began to stuff them
in the doorway.
"Wait a minute," Ma shouted.
"This house is occupied."
"Occupied by walnuts,"
answered the sharp-toothed squirrels.
And as Ma and Pa and Sam raced
for safety,
the bigger squirrel threw a walnut
at them.

They hid under a dry pea pod.
Pa thought a minute.

"If we clean out this pod,
we'll have a getaway boat."

With a stick for a mast
and Ma's skirt for a sail,
they floated down a clear stream.

"This is the life," sighed Ma.
"Where are we going?" asked Sam.

Just then the pod boat
got stuck between stones.
The sun was going down
and the sky above looked
empty and cold.

A turtle lifted a gray-wrinkled head.
"What will you give me if I save you?"
he asked slyly,
through half-closed eyelids.

"We'll give you a wish," said Pa.

"But a small one. I can do a bit of

magic. Nothing special.

Because of my size."

(Pa had pulled a flea out of a hat once.)

"Okay," muttered the turtle.

He carried them

to the other shore.

"Now for that wish," he said.

Pa, Ma, and Sam listened carefully.

"I've always wished..." whispered
the turtle. He looked embarrassed.

"Yes, you've always wished?" Ma asked.

"...For some warm boots for winter,"
he said in a small voice.

"That doesn't take magic.

That takes know-how," Ma replied.

And she set to work with Pa and Sam's help.

They knitted four fine boots
out of thistledown,
tying them on the turtle
with the thinnest grapevine.
He smiled gratefully
and slowly slip-slopped away.

"We must find a place to sleep
before the moon rolls out," Pa said.
"Other witches enjoy moonlight,
but it is not good for us."

Pa knew that owls' eyes see best at night.
"If only we had our broom, we could fly,"
said Ma. "Let's make a new one."
They found a strong twig and set to work.
When it was finished, they climbed aboard.

They whizzed through the dark, cold air
as the moon climbed higher in the sky.
Balancing and holding on to their hats
at the same time was not easy.
"I hope we find someplace to fit in soon,"
whispered Sam, shivering.

Just ahead Pa saw a small cottage
on the top of a high hill.
"The answer to our prayers,"
Pa said.
Inside the cottage lived an old man
named Mike Feeney.
His wife had been gone for many years.

He sat mending his wool stockings.
Two birds slept in a cage.
Sam and Pa and Ma flew in
through a crack in the wall.
A warm fire crackled in the hearth.

"We'll fit here," said Pa,
settling the broom down on a high shelf
next to a handsome teapot.

"The perfect place," he said,
eyeing the teapot.
While Ma and Pa got the teapot ready,

Sam flew off on the broom by himself.
He darted about the room, wobbling.
"There's an insect in here,"
shouted Mike, chasing Sam
with a flyswatter.

Poor Sam lost his balance
and tumbled onto the soft rag rug.
As fast as he could,
he crawled into a mousehole in the wall.

It was the home of
Elmer Harvest Mouse.
Like the old man,
Elmer was old but lively.
"Out! Out!" he squeaked.

Sam looked glum. "Not again,"
he said. "There is no place
for Ma and Pa and me. We don't
fit anywhere!"

"Young fellow, what kind of a mouse
are you?" Elmer asked.

"No mouse," Sam told him. "Just a misfit—
the world's tiniest witch."
"My, my," said Elmer.

"Listen. I don't get much company.
Tell your ma and pa to come and visit.
Any time."

Sam said thank you
and peeked out the hole.
Mike was asleep in a chair by the fire.
Sam raced up to the shelf.

"Where were you?" cried Ma and Pa.
"Hop inside."
That night, exhausted,
all three slept in their new house.

Early in the morning
Mike came whistling
toward the shelf.
He took down the teapot
and Ma Witch, Pa Witch, and Sam
all fell out.
"More flies!" yelled Mike.
"Pesky critters."

The Witches ran away
as fast as they could.
"Quick! Quick!"
squeaked Elmer Harvest Mouse.
"In here."
Ma and Pa introduced themselves
and Sam introduced Elmer.

The family spent a happy morning
listening to Elmer's tales of days
when he was a young Harvester.
Once he was almost caught by a gray cat
as he carried in kernels of corn.

Ma and Pa and Sam were fascinated.
They wanted to hear more,
but Elmer began to doze,
mumbling,
"More tomorrow."

The family tiptoed out
and began to look for a new house.
They found a worn slipper in the closet.
"I guess we fit here," grumbled Pa.
"Somehow I wanted something better."
They pushed the slipper
into the shadows and fixed it up.

Mike Feeney didn't mind
having a mouse in the house.
He left Elmer slices of cheese
and Elmer shared them with his new friends.
"That mouse eats more all the time,"
Mike said to himself one day.

Winter winds whirled about the cottage.
The best place to be was
in Elmer's snug mousehole,

listening to his stories.

But every night, when Elmer dozed off,

the tiny Witches crept away to their slipper.

Then, one very cold morning,
Mike wanted to wear his slippers.
He went to the closet and found one.
"Where is my other slipper?" he asked
out loud, and began looking for it.
The teeny tiny Witches
raced between his fingers
and fled to Elmer's mousehole.

"It's happened again," groaned Pa.
"We don't fit here either."
"Oh, yes you do," said Elmer.

"Where?" said Ma.
"Mike just took our slipper."
"Right here," said Elmer, smiling.
"Oh, we couldn't!" said Ma.
But the more she thought about it,
the better it sounded.

The mousehole did need a bit of fixing up.
And she knew where there were some
scraps of cloth.

She could make curtains, and pillows,
and cover Elmer's footstool…
"Oh, Elmer," said Ma.

Pa and Sam nodded.

Elmer grabbed his tail
and started dancing.

The teeny tiny Witches joined in.

They fitted somewhere.